Ocean Planet Adventure

Story by Phillip Simpson
Illustrations by Richard Hoit

Contents

Chapter 1

Welcome to Ocean Planet

The spaceship touched down on the landing pad at Ocean Planet.
Jake and Anna looked out the window.
The only thing they could see was water.
There was water everywhere!

"Wow," said Anna to her mum and dad.
"This is going to be so much fun!"

"Yes," said Jake.
"We'll get to see all the giant sea animals!"

The family had come to Ocean Planet for the weekend.
It was a special place because of all the amazing sea animals that lived there.

"Look over there!" said Anna. "It's a submarine.
We can take it to the hotel
at the bottom of the ocean."

The two children ran over to the submarine. It was bobbing up and down next to a sign that said "Ocean Planet Hotel".

"Come on, Mum and Dad," said Jake. "Hurry, let's go!"

Chapter 2

Into the Deep Ocean

Jake, Anna and their parents climbed into the submarine.

Mum sat in the driver's seat. In front of her were the controls and a big window.

"Which way is it to the hotel?" asked Dad.

Mum pointed to a screen in front of the controls.
It showed a red dot and a green dot.

"The green dot shows us where we are," said Mum.
"Ocean Planet Hotel is the red dot.
I just have to go towards the red dot."

"Do we know how to drive this submarine?" asked Dad.

"Oh, Dad. Didn't you read about the submarines at Ocean Planet?" said Anna.
"The controls are easy to use."

Jake closed the hatch.

The submarine started to sink below the surface of the water.

Chapter 3

A Huge Flipper!

Suddenly, a giant school of fish filled the window.

Then, the fish were pushed out of the way by a huge flipper!

The flipper hit the window.

A big crack appeared, and water began to pour into the submarine.

"What shall we do?" asked Dad, terrified.

"The hotel is nearby," said Mum.
"It's in the deep water below us."

"Will the submarine make it?" asked Jake.

Mum shook her head.
"I don't think so. We've got to get out."

Anna, Jake and Dad began to look around
the submarine for diving suits.
Anna saw a locker above her head and opened it.

"Here," she said, pulling out some diving suits.
"Everyone put one of these on."

Quickly, they all put the suits on.

Just in time! The window cracked apart and water flooded in.

Jake opened the hatch and they all swam out.

"Which way?" asked Dad.

"There!" said Anna, pointing.

Far below them, they could see the lights of the hotel.

Chapter 4

A Ride to Ocean Planet Hotel

Just then, a giant shape appeared
in front of the family.
It looked like a sea turtle,
but much, much bigger.

It was even bigger than the submarine.

The giant turtle bobbed up and down in front of them, as if it was waiting for them.

"What is it doing?" asked Mum.

"We've seen flippers like that before," said Anna.

"Yes, I think one of them hit our window," said Jake.

"Maybe the turtle is sorry
and it wants to help?" said Dad.

The turtle turned around,
as though it was showing the family its huge shell.

"I think it wants us to hop on!" said Anna.

All four of them grabbed onto the shell.

The turtle dived straight down.

"Yes!" shouted Jake, as they dived. "This is great!"

Within minutes, the turtle had reached the hotel. It swam up to the door of an airlock.

"Thanks for the lift!" said Anna.

The turtle seemed to nod, and then swam away.

"Well, if that's just the start,
we're going to have an exciting weekend!"
said Jake.

"I can't wait!" said Anna.